W9-AUK-755

Mr. Marty Loves a Party!

Dan Gutman

Pictures by Jim Paillot

HARPER

An Imprint of HarperCollinsPublishers

To Madeline Smith

My Weirder-est School #5: Mr. Marty Loves a Party!
Text copyright © 2020 by Dan Gutman
Illustrations copyright © 2020 by Jim Paillot
All rights reserved. Printed in the United States of America.

Library of Congress Control Number: 2019956230
ISBN 978-0-06-269113-2 (pbk bdg.) — ISBN 978-0-06-269114-9 (library bdg.)

Typography by Laura Mock
20 21 22 23 24   PC/LSCH   10 9 8 7 6 5 4 3 2 1
❖
First Edition

Contents

Happy Birthday to Me

My name is A.J. and I know what you're thinking. You're wondering why I just put four M&M's in my mouth.

Let me explain. If I put just one M&M in my mouth, I would barely taste it. The thing is just too small. It would be like taking a pill.

Two M&M's are twice as much as one

M&M, of course. But they're still not enough to get that full chocolate blast after you melt the candy coating in your mouth.

Three M&M's are almost enough. But when you put three M&M's in your mouth, you definitely feel like something is missing.

Four is the perfect number of M&M's to put in your mouth at one time. Yum!

If you put five M&M's in your mouth, well, they're not gonna taste any better than four M&M's. So why do it? And if you're one of those people who pop a whole handful of M&M's in your mouth at once, well, that's just crazy. What a waste of perfectly good M&M's.

So there you have it. Now you know that four is the magic number of M&M's to put in your mouth at one time. You're welcome.

"A.J.," my mom said, "the big day is coming. What do you want for your birthday?"

"A truck full of M&M's," I replied.

"You can't buy a truck full of M&M's," my dad told me.

Nine years old. That's a big one. This will be my last single-digit birthday. Once you hit ten years old, you're into double digits. And you know what that means—it's all downhill from there. Not many people live to be a hundred years old and reach triple digits. So once you reach double digits, your life is pretty much over. You might as well move to a nursing home.

"Seriously, A.J.," my dad asked, "what do you want for your birthday? Or what do you want to *do* for your birthday?"

"Can I take a trip to outer space?" I asked.

"There are no trips to outer space," my mom replied. "At least not yet."

"How about Antarctica?" I suggested. "I've always wanted to go to Antarctica and live with the penguins."

"That's a little too far away, A.J.," my dad said.

"Can I go bungee

jumping off the Empire State Building?" I asked.

Bungee jumping off the Empire State Building would be cool.

"I'm pretty sure that's not allowed," said my mom.

Parents are such a drag. They never let you do anything that's fun. I wasn't getting anywhere. I would have to ask for something smaller.

"How about a fireworks party?" I suggested. "Blowing stuff up is cool."

"I don't think our neighbors would appreciate that," said

my dad. "If we had a fireworks party, Mr. Floyd next door would probably call the police."

Bummer in the summer! No matter *what* I suggested, my parents came up with some lame reason why we couldn't do it. This was going to be the worst birthday in the history of birthdays.

"How about we just have a regular birthday party, A.J.?" suggested my mom. "We'll have all your friends over, and we'll have balloons and cake and games and—"

Ugh, I hate parties. Parties are boring. Last year, I went to the birthday party of this girl in my class named Andrea Young who's really annoying and has curly brown hair. It was a tea party. No kidding! I had to get all dressed up and sit around drinking tea with a bunch of Andrea's girly-girl friends. What a snoozefest.

"It will be fun, A.J.!" my mom continued. "In fact, I heard that one of my old friends from college is a party planner now."

"That's a job?" I asked.

I can't believe somebody spent four years in college and ended up planning parties. That party planner should get a real job.

"I've heard that he's very good," my mom said excitedly. "He's planned hundreds of fun and unusual parties for kids. Everybody in town hires him. I have his number. I can call him right now!"

"Isn't that going to be expensive?" I asked.

"This is your last single-digit birthday, A.J.," said my dad. "Money is no object."*

---

*Well, if it's not an object, what is it?

Talk to the Hand

The next day was Saturday, so I got to sleep late. Yay! No school! When I woke up and opened my window shades, I saw a blue minivan pull up in front of our house. On the side, it said . . .

That was weird.

"My old friend Marty is here!" Mom hollered. "I haven't seen him since college."

I came downstairs, and you'll never believe who walked through the door at that moment.

Nobody! You can't walk through a door. Doors are made out of wood. But you'll never believe who walked through the door*way*.

It was Mr. Marty, of course. You should have been able to guess that. Who else could it have been?

Mr. Marty looked pretty normal. Well, he did have a sock puppet on one hand. The puppet looked like a miniature version of Mr. Marty. But other than that, Mr. Marty seemed pretty normal. He stuck his puppet in my face.

"You must be the birthday boy!" the puppet said in a weird, high voice. "Is your name A.J.?"

My parents always tell me not to talk to strangers, especially strangers who have a puppet on their hand. But I figured it would be okay because Mr. Marty was my mom's old friend.

"Why are you wearing a sock on your hand?" I asked Mr. Marty.

"Just ignore that big guy behind me," said Mr. Marty's sock puppet. "Talk to the hand. My name is Mini-Marty, and I love a party!"

Mini-Marty?*

People who walk around with sock puppets of themselves are weird.

"I bet you're excited about your birthday

---

*Isn't that a place at a gas station that sells stuff?

coming up," said Mini-Marty.

"Yeah, I guess," I replied unexcitedly.

"I know what it's like," Mini-Marty said. "I was a boy once."

"Just once?" I replied. "I'm a boy all the time."

"Hey, that's a good one!" said Mini-Marty. Then the puppet let out a weird laugh even though I didn't say anything funny.

My mom came over to give Mr. Marty a hug. She pretended like it wasn't weird for Mr. Marty to walk around with a sock puppet of himself on his hand. She also gave him a cup of coffee, which is what grown-ups do. Anytime grown-ups come over to your house, they have to drink coffee together. That's the first rule of being a grown-up.

Mr. Marty drank the coffee using his non-puppet hand. Mini-Marty didn't drink any coffee.

I wondered if Mr. Marty ever took Mini-Marty off his hand. I mean, it would be hard to take a shower with a puppet on your hand. How would you soap yourself up?

"This is going to be your birthday party, A.J.," said Mini-Marty, "so you should make the important decisions. What kind of party do you want to have?"

"How about a skateboarding party?" I suggested.

"Hmmmm," all three grown-ups said at the same time. And you know what that means. It means I wasn't going to have a skateboarding party.

"There might be liability issues," said Mini-Marty.

I didn't know what that meant. But I figure "liability" means the ability to lie.

"How about a football party?" I suggested. "We could go out to the high school field with my friends and—"

"I don't think that's allowed," said my dad.

"Somebody could get hurt," added my mom.

"I thought *I* was going to make the important decisions," I reminded them.

"You are, sweetie," said my mom.

"Well," I said, "why don't you tell me what kind of party I can have?"

"Great idea! You came to the right place," said Mini-Marty even though I didn't go anywhere. "I've got hundreds of ideas for fun birthday parties."

Mr. Marty took out a thick three-ring binder and started leafing through the pages.

"Let's see," said Mini-Marty. "How about a clown party? I have two wonderful clowns on my list of contacts."

"Clowns are creepy," I said. "I don't want a clown."

I saw a movie once about a clown that murders everybody in the town. I didn't want some evil clown at my birthday party.

"No worries," said Mini-Marty, leafing through the pages. "How about a dance party? I know a terrific DJ."

"Oooh, I love dancing!" said my mom.

"I hate dancing," I said.

"How about a paint-your-own-pottery party?" said Mini-Marty. "Everybody gets a plate, and you and your friends get to decorate them."

"After we decorate them," I said, "do we get to smash them up into little pieces with sledgehammers?"

"Uh, no," said Mini-Marty. "That's not part of it."

"Well, then forget it," I said.

A paint-your-own-pottery party would only be cool if we got to smash the pottery with sledgehammers.

"How about a science party?" said Mini-Marty. "Mrs. Wizard does lots of fun experiments—"

"That sounds like school," I told him.

"Fair enough," said Mini-Marty. "How about a gymnastics party with Miss Tumbles? That's not like school. She's an amazing gymnast."

"I hate gymnastics," I said.

"A cooking party?" Mini-Marty suggested. "You and your friends can make a yummy meal together, and then you get to eat the food you made."

"Cooking parties are for girls," I told the puppet.

"That's ridiculous, A.J.," said my dad.

"Many of the top chefs in the world are men."

"Thank you. Next," I said.

All those parties sounded boring to me.

"Don't worry," said Mini-Marty as Mr. Marty kept flipping the pages in his binder. "We'll find something. I have about a hundred party entertainers on my email list. That's why everybody calls me 'Mr. Party.' Say . . . how about a Star Wars party?"

Star Wars is cool. All my friends love Star Wars. I saw the last Star Wars movie a million hundred times.

"Tell me more," I said.

"I know a guy who has a Darth Vader costume," said Mini-Marty. "He comes

over to your house and shows all the kids
how to use a lightsaber. It's quite a show."

"Isn't that dangerous?" asked my mom.

"No, it's perfectly safe," said Mini-Marty.

"Okay, let's go with that," I said.

"Consider it done!" said Mini-Marty. "We'll have the best Star Wars party ever!"

"I can bake a batch of Star Wars cookies for the kids," said my mom.

"Don't bother with food," said Mini-Marty. "I'll take care of everything—the food, the music, the entertainment. Leave it to me. All you have to do is be here on the big day. Mr. Marty loves a party!"

Then he left. This was going to be the greatest birthday party in the history of the world.

Because I Said So

That night, my parents called me over to the kitchen table for a big meeting. My dad had a pen and one of those yellow legal pads* in front of him.

"We need to make the invitation list for your birthday party, A.J.," said my mom. "Let's start with Grandma and Grandpa . . ."

---

*I guess it's illegal to use a pad that's not yellow.

"And Aunt Lucy and Uncle Jerry, of course," my dad said as he wrote their names on his yellow legal pad.

I guess you have to invite your relatives to your party. I mean, if it wasn't for your grandparents, your parents wouldn't have been born. And if it wasn't for your parents, you wouldn't have been born. And if you're not born, you don't even get a birthday party. That's why it's called a birthday.

"Which of the kids at school do you want to invite?" asked my mom.

"Ryan, Michael, and Neil are my best friends," I said.

"You can't just have boys at your birthday party, A.J.," my mom told me.

"Why not?" I asked.

"Because I said so," replied both of my parents.

Only parents can get away with saying "because I said so." I can't wait until I'm a parent so I can tell my kids "because I said so" and not give them any reason why.

"Okay," I said. "I'll invite Alexia too. She's a girl, and she's cool."

Dad wrote ALEXIA JUAREZ on his yellow legal pad.

"What about Andrea Young?" asked my mom.

Ugh! Gross.

I didn't want to invite Smarty Pants, Little Miss Perfect, the Human Homework Machine to my birthday party. That try-hard, know-it-all Andrea would ruin all the fun.

"A.J., we *have* to invite Andrea," said my mom.

"Why?"

"Because she invited you to her birthday party last year," Mom replied. "So you have to invite her to yours. That's only fair."

"No, it's not!" I shouted. "If she invited me to her funeral, would that mean I would have to invite her to my funeral?"

"People don't invite each other to their own funerals," my dad told me.

"See? That's exactly what I mean!" I said.

"If Andrea's mother finds out we had a

birthday party and didn't invite Andrea, she'd be very upset," my mom explained. "She and I play tennis together every week."

I didn't see what tennis had to do with my birthday party. That didn't make any sense.

I looked at my dad with my best puppy-dog face. If I could get him on my side, it would be possible for me to win the argument.

Divide and conquer. That's the first rule of winning an argument with your parents. And always put on your best puppy-dog face.

"A.J., we have to invite Andrea," said my dad.

Oh, well. So much for that idea. Dad wrote ANDREA YOUNG on his yellow legal pad.

"If we invite Andrea," said my mom, "we have to invite Emily."

WHAT?! Emily is Andrea's little cry-baby friend, and she's equally annoying.

"Why do we have to invite Emily?" I shouted. "You don't play tennis with Emily's mother."

"Andrea and Emily are best friends," my mom explained. "It wouldn't be right to invite Andrea to your party and not invite Emily. It would hurt Emily's feelings."

"So let's not invite either of them!" I said.

Dad wrote EMILY on his yellow legal pad. Then he asked, "What about Mr. Cooper?"

"Oh yes!" agreed my mom. "Mr. Cooper has been so nice to you this year."

WHAT?! I don't want my teacher to be at my birthday party! He would spend the whole time telling us to stop talking and line up in size order.

"Why would Mr. Cooper want to come

to a Star Wars party?" I asked.

At that point, my parents were just ignoring me.

". . . and Mr. Klutz and Mrs. Roopy and Ms. Hannah and Miss Small . . ."

Dad wrote a bunch more names on the yellow legal pad.

This party was going to be the worst thing to happen since National Poetry Month! I wanted to go run away to Antarctica and live with the penguins.

May the Force Be with You

It felt like a million hundred days until my birthday finally arrived.

It was a sunny day, so that meant we could have the party in our backyard instead of inside the house. Yay! Outdoor birthday parties are way more fun than indoor birthday parties. That's the first rule of birthday parties.

About nine o'clock in the morning, a truck came and dropped off three porta potties in our backyard. It didn't occur to me that if you're going to have a bunch of people over to your house, you're going to need more bathrooms.

"Wow, I'm glad we hired Mr. Marty," said my mom. "He thinks of everything. That's why he's the number one party planner in the area."

"I guess he's also the number two party planner in the area," my dad said. Then he started cracking up even though he didn't say anything funny.

The porta potty said "MR. JOHN" on it. My parents told me that toilets used to be called "johns." Nobody knows why.

I'm just glad my name isn't John, because then it would be like I was a toilet.

Soon the doorbell rang. My mom went to answer it. And you'll never believe who poked his head into the door at that moment.

Nobody! Poking your head into a door would hurt. I thought we went over that in Chapter 2.

But you'll never believe who poked his head into the doorway.

It was Mr. Marty. He had the Mini-Marty sock puppet on his hand, of course.

"Happy birthday, A.J!" said Mini-Marty. "You're going to have a fabulous party. Are you folks excited? This is going to be amazing! Darth Vader will be here any minute. The pizza should be here at noon. Blah blah blah blah blah blah blah blah blah blah blah blah blah . . ."

He went on like that for a while. Mr. Marty gave my parents some papers to sign, and they gave him a credit card to pay for the party. While they were doing that, the doorbell rang again.

"I'll get it!" I yelled. "It's probably Ryan, Michael, and Neil."

But it wasn't my friends. You'll never believe who walked into the door at that moment.

Nobody! Aren't you paying attention? We just discussed this a few sentences ago! But you'll never believe who walked into the door*way*.

It was Darth Vader! Yes! The real Darth Vader!

Well, Darth Vader is just a character in the movies, so there's no real Darth Vader. But it was a guy in a real Darth Vader costume, and that's pretty cool. He was tall and scary looking, and he had his lightsaber with him. I couldn't believe the famous Darth Vader was standing right in front of me, staring me in the face.

"Happy birthday," Darth Vader said in a plain old regular guy's voice. "Can I use your bathroom?"*

Wow! Darth Vader wanted to use our bathroom. I was speechless.

---

*Ha! And you thought there would be no toilet jokes in this book.

"It's kind of an emergency," he added.

"Uh, yeah, sure," I told him. "The bathroom is down the hall, to the right."

"Thanks," he replied. "I might be in there for a while, if you know what I mean."

Darth Vader rushed down the hall to the bathroom and shut the door behind him.

That was cool. In the Star Wars movies, Darth Vader *never* goes to the bathroom. In fact, nobody ever goes to the bathroom in the Star Wars movies. I guess they just hold it in. I don't even know if they *have* bathrooms on spaceships.

"Was that your friends at the door, sweetie?" called my mom.

"No, it was Darth Vader," I told her. "He's in the bathroom. He told me it was an emergency."

"Gee, I hope he's okay," said my dad.

"Don't worry," said Mini-Marty. "I'm sure he'll be fine."

After a few minutes, the doorbell rang again. It was my best friends Ryan, Michael, and Neil.

"Happy birthday, dude!" shouted Ryan, who will eat anything, even stuff that isn't food.

"Happy birthday, dude!" shouted Michael, who never ties his shoes.

"Happy birthday, dude!" shouted Neil, who we call the nude kid even though he wears clothes.

Each of them handed me a present. I wanted to tear off the wrapping paper right away, but my mom told me to put the presents in the corner and we'd open them after the party was over. Bummer in the summer!

A few minutes later, the doorbell rang again. It was Andrea and Emily. Ugh.

"Happy birthday to you . . ." they sang. "Happy birthday to you . . ."

Andrea and Emily had to sing the whole happy birthday song. They are so annoying. I told them they could go in the backyard.

"What is Andrea doing here?" asked Neil.

"I had to invite her," I explained. "My parents made me."

"Ooooh," Ryan said. "A.J. invited Andrea to his birthday party. They must be in LOVE!"

"When are you going to get married?" asked Michael.

If those guys weren't my best friends, I would hate them.

"Where's Darth Vader?" asked Michael.

"Yeah, I thought this was going to be a Star Wars party," said Ryan.

"He's in the bathroom," I told them. "I better go check on him. You guys can go in the backyard."

I went over to the bathroom door.

"Are you okay in there, Mr. Vader?" I asked.

"I'm . . . just a little, uh . . . blocked up," he replied.

I know what that means. Darth Vader was constipated. Grown-ups think the word "constipated" is disgusting, so they say "blocked up" instead. Nobody knows why.

"You should use the Force," I suggested.

"Very funny," Darth Vader replied. "Leave me alone."

The doorbell rang again. There were a bunch of people outside—Alexia, Mr. Klutz, my grandparents, my aunt and

uncle, Mr. Cooper, and some of the other teachers from school. All of them brought presents. I'm glad I let my parents talk me into inviting so many people. The more people you invite to your party, the more presents you get.

I led them all out to the backyard. Everyone stood around making chitchat. Chitchat is what you say when you don't have anything to talk about. I hate making chitchat.

Andrea started chitchatting with my grandmother, and it took about five seconds for her to convince Grandma that she was the sweetest little girl in the world. Ugh.

The party was already boring. I went over to Mr. Marty, who was chitchatting with my dad.

"What are we going to do?" I asked him. "Darth Vader is supposed to be teaching us how to use lightsabers, but he's in the bathroom. Nobody has anything to do. They're just standing around making chitchat."

"I'm sure Darth will be out any minute," said Mini-Marty. "He's a professional. Just relax, talk to your friends, and stop worrying so much. It's your birthday!"

"Darth Vader should have more bran in his diet," said my mom, who thinks everybody should have more bran in their diet.

"No, he needs more fiber," said Mr. Klutz. "Fiber keeps you regular."

"And fruit," added my dad. "You've got to eat a lot of fruit, so you won't get blocked up."

Ugh. The grown-ups spent the next five minutes arguing about the best way to prevent constipation. It was a chitchat snoozefest.

That's when the weirdest thing in the history of the world happened.

But I'm not going to tell you what it was.

Okay, okay, I'll tell you. But you have to read the next chapter. So nah-nah-nah boo-boo on you!

A Lucky Mistake

Everybody was in the backyard. It was looking like my party was going to be the biggest disaster since the *Titanic* hit that iceberg. Everybody was standing around chitchatting. Darth Vader was still in the bathroom. There wasn't anything to eat. The pizza guy wouldn't be there for an hour.

Suddenly, there was a knocking sound on our backyard gate.

"Who could that be?" asked my mom. "All the guests have arrived."

"Maybe the pizza guy is here early," said my dad.

But it wasn't the pizza guy. My mom and I opened the gate, and a guy was standing there. He had a painted white face, frizzy red hair, a red nose, giant shoes, and a silly costume with red polka dots all over it. He was carrying a big sack.

It was a clown! Clowns are so creepy. I fell back in horror.

"I'm Buffo the Clown," the clown said. "You must be the birthday boy."

"We didn't order a clown," my mom told him.

"Mr. Marty sent me an email," Buffo the Clown replied. "It said to be here at eleven o'clock. It's eleven o'clock."

"There must be some mistake," my mom said.

Mr. Marty came running over.

"Buffo!" Mini-Marty said excitedly. "So good to see you. I'm so sorry. I must have emailed you by accident. But what a lucky mistake! I'm so glad you're here. Darth Vader is supposed to be entertaining the kids, but he's in the bathroom."

"This is perfect!" my mom said excitedly. "You saved the party, Buffo!"

Suddenly, I wasn't having a Star Wars party anymore. I was having a Buffo the Clown party.

Oh, well. That had to be better than a bunch of people standing around making chitchat for hours.

"Wait a minute," said Buffo. "Am I gonna get paid for this gig?"

"Of course," replied Mini-Marty. "Don't worry about it."

"Then let the Buffo the Clown show begin!" announced Buffo.

He ran into the middle of the backyard, honking a horn that was attached to his belt.

"Hey, kids!" shouted Buffo. "Do you wanna hear a joke?"

"Yeah!" we all shouted.

"I CAN'T HEAR YOU!" said Buffo.

Entertainers are always saying they can't hear you even after you just shouted at them. They must need hearing aids.

"YEAH!" we all shouted louder.

"What's black and white and red all over?" asked Buffo.

"A newspaper!" somebody shouted.

"No!" said Buffo.

"An embarrassed nun!" somebody shouted.

"No!"

"A sunburned zebra!" somebody shouted.

"No!" said Buffo. "It's a polar bear eating a penguin!"

"Oh, snap!" said Ryan.

Everybody laughed except Andrea, who said that the joke was violent and inappropriate for children.* I didn't think Buffo's joke was all that funny, but jokes always sound funnier when they're told by a guy in a clown costume.

Buffo the Clown told a few more bad jokes. Then he juggled balls, played the kazoo, sang some silly songs, and made balloon animals for all of us. He was actually pretty entertaining, and he didn't even murder anybody, as far as I know. Maybe I should rethink my opinion of clowns.

---

*Send your complaints to www.getasenseofhumor.transplant.

"Hey, Buffo the Clown is cool," said Ryan.

"Great party, dude," Alexia told me.

While Buffo was making a giant balloon hat for Andrea, there was a knock on the gate.

"That must be the pizza guy!" Neil shouted.

"Yay!" yelled Michael. "I'm starved."

But it wasn't the pizza guy.

You'll never believe who was standing there when I opened the gate.

It was another clown!

"Who are you?" I asked.

"I'm Giggles the Clown," said the clown. "Are you the birthday boy? I got an email from Mr. Marty telling me to come to this address. I got a little lost on the way over. Sorry I'm late."

"We already have a clown," I told him.

"What?!" shouted Giggles. "It's not Buffo the Clown, is it?"

"Actually, it is."

"I hate Buffo!" muttered Giggles. He marched into the middle of the backyard, looking really angry.

"Buffo!" shouted Giggles.

"Giggles!" shouted Buffo.

"So . . . we meet again," said Giggles.

"We're going to have a problem here," Buffo announced. "There can't be two clowns at the same party."

That must be the first rule of being a clown.

"We didn't invite *any* clowns," said my dad.

But Buffo and Giggles weren't paying attention. They just glared at each other, like two wild animals in the jungle.

"I told you to stay out of my territory, Giggles," said Buffo. "This is *my* party, and this is the second time this month you tried to steal my gig."

"It's *my* gig," replied Giggles.

"Mine!"

"Mine!"

They went on like that for a while. That's when the weirdest thing in the history of the world happened. Giggles tried to punch Buffo, but he missed and fell on the ground. It was actually pretty funny.

Everybody laughed. Then Giggles got up and squirted Buffo in the face with a fake flower.

"Oh, I get it!" said my grandma. "They do a comedy clown act! How charming!"

"It's adorable!" said my mom.

That's what we all thought. But then Buffo took a swing at Giggles and socked him hard, right in the jaw. Giggles staggered backward, holding his mouth. Then he charged at Buffo and wrestled him to the ground.

"Clown fight!" shouted Michael.

Giggles and Buffo started rolling around on the grass, shouting and grabbing each other.

"I don't approve of this violence," said Andrea.

"What do you have against violins?" I asked her.

"Not violins, Arlo! Violence!"

A Knock on the Gate

All the grown-ups rushed over to break up the fight between the two clowns. That's when the weirdest thing in the history of the world happened.

There was another knock on the gate. I thought it was going to be the pizza guy, or maybe another clown. But it wasn't the pizza guy or another clown. I opened the gate, and there were two truck drivers standing there.

"To what do we owe the pleasure of your company?" I asked. That's how grown-ups say "What are *you* doing here?"

"We're here to deliver the giant inflatable bouncy castle," one of the truck drivers said.

I looked behind them. There was a truck parked in the driveway with one of those giant inflatable bouncy castles on it. It was already inflated.

"HUH?" I said, which is also "HUH" backward. "We didn't order a giant inflatable bouncy castle."

"Well, I got an email from Mr. Marty telling us to deliver a giant inflatable bouncy
castle to this address," the guy said.

"There must be some mistake," I said in
my best talking-to-grown-ups voice.

"Hey, that ain't my problem, kid," said

the other truck driver. "We just make the deliveries. Where do you want it?"

"Put it over there," I said, pointing to the corner of the backyard.

They carried in the giant inflatable bouncy castle. All the kids ran over and jumped on it.

"Whee!" shouted Alexia. "Bouncy castles are cool!"

The truck drivers left, and a few minutes later there was *another* knock on the gate. I ran over to open it. There was a guy pulling a big suitcase on wheels. He was wearing a backward baseball cap and sunglasses.

"I'm DJ Jazzy Jim," he told me. "I work

for Musical Munchkins. Where should I set up my stuff?"

"We didn't hire a DJ," I told him.

"Why not?" he said. "You can't have a party without music."

"Okay," I told him. "You can set your stuff up in that corner over there."

A few minutes later, there was another knock on the gate. I opened it, and a lady with pigtails was doing jumping jacks.

"Hi!" she said. "I'm Miss Tumbles from KinderGym. Is this the gymnastics party?"

"It is now," I told her. "Come on in."

When my dad saw DJ Jazzy Jim and Miss Tumbles come into the backyard, he marched over to Mr. Marty.

"What's going on?" my dad demanded. "We didn't invite these people to the party."

"Uhhhhhh," Mini-Marty said as Mr. Marty looked at his smartphone, "I seem to have made a little mistake. I think I may have emailed everyone on my client list by accident."

"WHAT?!" my dad shouted. "You made

a *little* mistake? How much is this going to cost me?"

"You said money was no object," Mini-Marty replied.

I looked over at the gate. There were a bunch of other people lined up there. Some of them were wearing costumes.

"Who are you?" I asked them.

"Is this the dance party?" said a lady wearing a tutu. "I'm Miss Donna, and I teach ballet, hip-hop, and tap dancing. I also give Zumba lessons."

I had no idea what Zumba was, but I let her in anyway.

"Bonjour!" said some guy with a beret on his head. "I am here to teach the children

how to speak French."

"Come on in," I told him.

Two guys were carrying a huge cardboard box that said GRAVITY IS FOR LOSERS on it.

"We're from Vertical Reality," one of them said. "Where do you want us to put the trampoline?"

"In that corner over there," I told them.

We were running out of corners for people to set up their stuff.

The next person was a lady wearing a T-shirt that said ABRACADOODLE PAINT YOUR OWN POTTERY on it. "I'm here for the arty party," she said. "Every child can be an artist!"

"We're here from the Fencing Academy," said a man and a lady wearing weird masks on their faces.

"We already have a fence," I told them. "You're standing right next to it."

"Not *that* kind of fencing," the man said. "We teach children how to duel."

Then the two of them whipped out swords, jumped into a pose, and shouted "en garde!" Whatever *that* means. They

started sword fighting. It was cool, so I let them in.

The line of people at the gate was getting longer.* My dad ran over to see what was going on. He looked pretty upset.

"Hello!" said a guy wearing a park ranger uniform. He had two big birds perched on his hands. "I'm Ranger Rick from the Wildlife Conservation Center, and these are birds of prey. I call them my party animals. Aren't they beautiful?"

"Get out of here!" my dad shouted at the guy. "We've got enough problems without birds flying around here."

"But they're endangered," the guy from

---

*Don't you wish you had a birthday party like this one?

the Wildlife Conservation Center said, making a puppy-dog face.

"Okay, okay," my dad grumbled, rubbing his forehead with his fingers. "Come on in."

Calm Down

They just kept coming, one after the other! There was a face painter, a bubble blower, a guy dressed like a ninja, a guy who looked like Frankenstein, two martial artists, and some lady named Mrs. Wizard who said she builds robots out of Legos. The backyard was jammed with all kinds of party entertainers. I let them all in. There was no stopping them.

Suddenly, I remembered that Darth Vader was still in the bathroom. He had been there for about a million hundred hours. I was starting to get worried. I ran inside the house and went over to the bathroom door.

"Is everything okay in there, Mr. Vader?" I asked. "Can I get you anything?"

"Just leave me alone," he shouted. "I'll be out soon."

I went back to the party. Everybody seemed to be having a good time. People were painting their own pottery, jumping on the trampoline, and dancing to DJ Jazzy Jim's music. My grandmother was learning how to Zumba, whatever that is.

"You sure know how to throw a party, A.J.!" Ryan shouted over the music.

"Yeah, but I'm starving," hollered Neil. "When is the pizza guy going to show up?"

"Good question," I replied.

At that point, I noticed some guy standing over by the gate.

"That must be the pizza guy!" I shouted.

"At last!" everybody yelled.

Mr. Marty and my dad went to the gate.

But it wasn't the pizza guy. It was a guy wearing a top hat and a black cape.

"Who are *you*?" my dad asked angrily.

"It is I, the Amazing Tortolini!" the guy announced as he pulled out a deck of cards. "Pick a card, any card!"

"Can you make all these people

disappear?" muttered my dad. "You might as well come in. Everybody else is here."

Right behind the Amazing Tortolini was a guy dressed as a cowboy and holding a guitar.

"Who are *you*?" my dad asked.

"Ah am Drusty Rhodes, the Singin' Cowpoke," the guy said, really slowly.

"Did you say Dusty or Rusty?" I asked.

"It's Drusty," he replied. "Ah came to strum a few tunes for the young 'uns." Then he started to sing . . .

"The ants are my friends, blowin' in the wind . . ."

Oh no, not *that* song! Why would anybody make friends with ants?

My dad grabbed Mr. Marty.

"When is your pizza guy going to get here?" Dad demanded. "The guests are complaining that they're starving."

"Hmmmm," Mini-Marty said as Mr.

Marty scrolled through the emails on his smartphone. "It looks like I made another tiny mistake. I may have forgotten to contact the pizza guy."

"WHAT?!" my dad shouted. "You emailed all these other people, but you forgot to order the pizza?"

My dad slammed the gate shut. His face was all red. It looked like he was going to explode. My mom came running over and put her arm around him.

"Calm down, honey," she said. "It will be okay. Everybody seems to be having a good time. That's the important thing, right?"

"I will *not* calm down!" Dad said, turning

to Mr. Marty. "I thought you were the number one party planner in town! I thought you were going to handle *everything*! You said we didn't have to do *anything*. That's what you told us. Remember?"

"Hey, it's not my fault," said Mini-Marty. "I'm just a puppet."

"What is your problem?" my dad shouted at Mr. Marty. "Normal people don't talk through puppets all the time!"

"I'm terribly sorry about the party," explained Mr. Marty. "It was a mistake. This has *never* happened before. What can I say? I told you I was sorry!"

"You're sorry? Well, I'm sorry, too!" shouted my dad. "I'm sorry that we don't have any food for our guests. I'm sorry that my backyard is filled with a bunch of nutjobs and I'm going to have to pay them all. I'm sorry that the only entertainer I hired has been in the bathroom for the whole party. I'm sorry that you ruined my son's birthday! This is the last straw!"*

That's when the coolest thing in the history of the world happened. My dad ripped the Mini-Marty puppet off Mr. Marty's hand and threw it over the fence!

(The puppet, that is. It would have been weird if he threw Mr. Marty's *hand* over the fence.)

---

*What did straws have to do with anything? And why are people always running out of them?

I looked at Mr. Marty. Mr. Marty looked at my mom. My mom looked at my dad. My dad looked at me. I looked at Mr. Marty. We were all looking at each other. I thought Mr. Marty might start crying

because he lost his Mini-Marty sock puppet. But he didn't have the chance because there was another knock at the gate.

"Oh *no!*" my dad hollered. "What *now*?"

He yanked open the gate so hard, I thought he might rip it off the hinges. A lady was standing there. She was wearing an apron and holding a spatula.

"Cheerio!" she said in a happy British accent. "I'm Miss Maggie from the Great British Cook-Off School. Is this a party for a young gentleman named A.J.?"

"GET *OUT!*" my dad screamed at her.

"Well, I *never!*" Miss Maggie said, backing away from the gate. "You are a rather rude man! I wouldn't want to attend this party anyway. Hmmmfff!"

She turned on her heel and was about to leave when my mom came running over.

"Miss Maggie! Miss Maggie!" she shouted. "Did you say you're with a cooking school?"

"Yes," Miss Maggie replied. "I was going to make pizzas with the children, but this mean man—"

"Come on in!" shouted my mom, pulling Miss Maggie into the backyard.

We brought in Miss Maggie's supplies and set up a make-your-own-pizza station on the porch near the kitchen. Miss Maggie had like a million hundred toppings, and we could put whatever we wanted on our pizzas. She had enough for everybody. It was awesome.

Mr. Marty couldn't stop saying "thank you" to Miss Maggie. She saved the party.

We were all eating our pizzas when there was *another* knock on the gate.

"Who in the blazes would be showing up *now*?" Mr. Marty asked. His hair and clothes were all messed up. It looked like he'd been through a war.

I know what you're thinking. You're thinking it was the pizza guy. It would be funny if the pizza guy finally showed up after we already ate our pizzas.

But it *wasn't* the pizza guy. So nah-nah-nah boo-boo on you!

Dad went over and opened the gate. A truck driver was standing there. The truck behind him in the driveway looked like one of those giant cement mixers.

"What do *you* want?" my dad asked angrily.

"Did somebody here order a truck full of M&M's?" asked the driver.

"Yes!" I shouted.

"This is the place, fellas!" hollered the

truck driver. "Back it up!"

Then he unloaded about a million hundred tons of M&M's.

This was the greatest birthday party in the history of birthday parties.

Make a Wish!

Everybody was having a great time bouncing on the bouncy castle, sword fighting, painting pottery, doing gymnastics, learning how to speak French, and stuffing their faces with M&M's. That's when I heard somebody start to sing "Happy Birthday." I looked over and saw my parents coming out of the kitchen with a birthday cake. It was huge, and there were nine candles stuck in it.

Happy birthday to you.
Happy birthday to you.
Happy birthday, dear A.J.
Happy birthday to you.

"Make a wish, sweetie!" shouted my mom.

Hmmmm, a wish. Choosing a wish is hard. There were so many things I could wish for. I tried to think. If I could have anything in the world, what would I want?

I could wish that school would be

declared illegal. That would be a good wish. I could wish for a new football. I could wish for a million hundred dollars so I could buy anything in the world. I could wish for more wishes, of course.

I was faced with the hardest decision of my life. I was concentrating so hard that my brain hurt.

"Just *one* wish, A.J.!" shouted my dad. Everybody laughed.

"Yeah, save a few wishes for next year," shouted my grandma.

Hmmmm. I could wish for a new skateboard. I could wish for a new video game. I could wish for Andrea to have a truck full of elephants fall on her head.

Nah, I decided to wish for school to be declared illegal. That would make me the happiest.

I took a deep breath and blew out all nine candles on the cake. That's when the weirdest thing in the history of the world happened.*

---

*Pretty short chapter, huh? If your parents say you have to read a chapter in a book every night, read this one.

The Big Surprise Ending

9

I know what you're thinking. You're thinking that when I blew out the candles, something caught on fire. You're thinking that set off a whole chain of events that ended with everybody running around yelling and screaming and hooting and hollering and freaking out.

Well, you're *wrong*! You think you know

so much? That's not at all what happened. So nah-nah-nah boo-boo on you. Here's what *really* happened . . .

I blew out all nine candles on my birthday cake, and everybody cheered. My mom cut the cake and started passing out pieces.

Everybody was having such a good time that they didn't want to leave. So they kept on jumping on the trampoline, painting pottery, singing songs, blowing bubbles, and getting their faces painted. The backyard was still crowded with people.

My grandmother was doing Zumba, whatever that is, and she must have tripped or something. She bumped into Ranger Rick from the Wildlife Conservation Center. That startled one of his birds of prey, which flew around crazily.

The bird smashed into the guy from the Fencing Academy, who fell down.

As he was falling, his sword went flying out of his hand. It landed right in the middle of the giant inflatable bouncy castle, poking a hole in it.

Psssssssssssss . . .

Air was escaping from the giant inflatable bouncy castle! It started to collapse!

Mrs. Wizard ran over with some duct tape to patch the hole in the giant inflatable bouncy castle. But on the way over, she bumped into the paint-your-own-pottery table.

All the pottery went flying! Some of the pieces hit Buffo the Clown. He thought Giggles the Clown was throwing pottery at him, and he became furious. The two of them started fighting again.

They knocked over DJ Jazzy Jim's speaker system. It landed on the Amazing Tortolini. He started crying.

Miss Tumbles and Drusty Rhodes ran over to help the Amazing Tortolini. Everybody else started running around yelling and screaming and hooting and hollering and freaking out.

"Run for your lives!" shouted Neil the nude kid.

You should have been there! I saw it with my own eyes!

Well, it would be pretty hard to see something with somebody else's eyes.

"Great party, A.J.!" Ryan said as we sat on the steps and ate birthday cake while we watched everybody going crazy.

"Best party *ever*," said Michael.

In the middle of all this, there was a knock on the gate.

"Who could *that* be?" asked my dad as he opened the gate.

There was a policeman standing there. He looked pretty mad. Mr. Marty came running over.

"My name is Officer Luke," the policeman said, flashing his badge.

"There must be some mistake," said Mr. Marty. "I didn't hire a guy dressed up as a policeman."

"I'm not dressed up as a policeman," said Officer Luke. "I *am* a policeman. There have been complaints from your neighbor Mr. Floyd about the noise. This party is disturbing the peace. Who's in charge here?"

I looked at my dad. My dad looked at my mom. My mom looked at Mr. Marty. Mr. Marty looked at Officer Luke. Everybody was looking at everybody else. Nobody was stepping forward to admit they were in charge.

I thought my dad was gonna die. After everything else that happened, now he might get arrested. He might have to go to jail for disturbing the peace!

"I . . . CAN'T . . . HEAR . . . YOU!" said Officer Luke. "I said who's in charge here?"

That's when the weirdest thing in the history of the world happened.

"I am!" somebody hollered. "I'm in charge!"

We all turned around. And you'll never believe in a million hundred years who came out of the house.

It was Darth Vader!

"Gasp!" everybody gasped as Darth Vader walked across the backyard, just like he does in the movies. Everybody stepped aside to let him through. It was cool.

"*You're* in charge?" asked Officer Luke, the policeman.

"That's right," said Darth Vader. "What's the problem?"

"This party is out of control," said the officer. "You're under arrest for disturbing the peace."

"You can't arrest me," said Darth Vader.

"Oh, yeah? Why not?"

Darth Vader paused for a ridiculously long time.

"Luke," he finally said. "I am . . . your father."

"Very funny," said Officer Luke.

That's when the weirdest thing in the history of the world happened. Darth Vader took off his Darth Vader helmet.

"Dad!" shouted Officer Luke. "You never told me you dressed up as Darth Vader! I thought you were a real estate salesman."

"I do this in my spare time," said Darth Vader. "That's how I was able to earn enough money to put you through the police academy."

Then Officer Luke and his dad hugged, and everybody clapped. My mom started crying.

Well, that's pretty much what happened.

Mr. Marty thanked everybody for coming to the party and apologized for emailing all of his clients by accident. We gave Officer Luke a piece of cake to show our appreciation, and Miss Donna offered to give him a free Zumba lesson, whatever that is.

After everybody went home, I opened my presents. Ryan got me a new football. Michael got me a new skateboard. Neil got me a new video game. I got lots of other cool stuff too.

I also got some lame presents, like clothes. Why would anybody give clothes as a birthday present? You can't do anything with them except wear them. I had to pretend I liked all the presents, because

that's the first rule of getting presents. It was kind of a drag writing all those thank-you notes to everybody. But all in all, I have to say it was the greatest day in my life.

Maybe the pizza guy will finally show up. Maybe Mr. Marty will get his Mini-Marty hand puppet back. Maybe Darth Vader will put more bran in his diet. Maybe I'll eat the whole truck full of M&M's. Maybe school will be declared illegal. Maybe my grandma will become a Zumba instructor. Maybe I'll be able to talk my parents into hiring Mr. Marty again for my birthday party next year.

But it won't be easy!*

---

*Hey, the book is finished. Why are you still hanging around? Go read something else.